Rockets

Mouse Magic

Wendy Smith

A & C Black • London

for Dorothy

Rockets

MRS MAGIC - Wendy Smith

Circle Magic

Crazy Magic

Magic Hotel

Mouse Magic

First paperback published 2000
First published 2000 in hardback by
A & C Black (Publishers) Ltd
35 Bedford Row, London WC1R 4JH

ISBN 0-7136-5330-2

A CIP catalogue record for this book is available from the British Library.

Printed and bound by G. Z. Printek, Bilbao, Spain.

Chapter One

Mrs Magic ran the Black Bat Hotel. Puss and Partridge helped her make it a place full of fun and magic.

But Mrs Magic was becoming tired of her job.

So, Mrs Magic went on a high altitude flight for a good long think. Eventually, she hatched a plan.

Puss and Partridge didn't like it when Mrs Magic flew above 1500 feet.

That night Puss could not sleep.

Partridge had a terrible nightmare.

So it was a relief when Mrs Magic revealed her plan.

Chapter Two

The next day, two huge lorries delivered eighty-eight computers, one for each room in the hotel.

Unfortunately, nobody knew what to do next.

Just then one of the guests walked by.

Mrs Magic asked Puss to make a program.

After a great deal of whirring the computer came to life.

The computer crackled and a Menu appeared on screen.

Magical Menu

1 for spells

2 for flying

3 for special effects inside room

4 for special effects outside room

5 for SURPRISE

6 for drinks

7 for food

Charlie showed everyone how to use the Magic Mouse.

And wow! The whole of the ground floor of the hotel turned into a toy shop.

The kids are going to love this.
And so am I.

Chapter Three

Of course, Partridge was absolutely right, the children did love the new computer magic.

① Spells
Here's a spell
to bring you a thrill,
Just turn and look
at your window sill.

Everybody had their own favourite spell.
Each one had a special magic.

The flying spell was especially good.

And families took to it very well.

Number three was always exciting.

Number four was great at night.

With five you never knew what kind of surprise to expect.

Numbers six and seven were particularly popular.

The adults loved the computers just as much.

Chapter Four

Why was it, then, that Mrs Magic began to miss the days before computers?

Puss and Partridge had hardly anything to do.

There were no spells.

No flying for Puss.

They began to sit around doing nothing.

And put on weight.

The hotel was eerily quiet.

I wonder if I can still do my toad spell.
How does it go?
Toadie. Toadie.
Toad... Oh. I know.
Toad of morning, Toad of night Bathe me in Some rainbow light.
You what?
pink
pink
yellow
yellow
pi
pin
yello
yellov
pink
pink
Not so good as I was.
croak

Mrs Magic wanted company.

Mrs Magic was not at all happy with the way things were going.

She went for a high altitude flight for a think. It took longer than usual, but at last she came up with a plan.

Chapter Five

By now the Black Bat Hotel was completely full.

In every room someone was using a computer.

Up in the Tower, the
surprise spell had
made a pirate ship.
There were only
two children to
make up
the crew.

It's my turn to walk the plank.

Since no one ever came out of their rooms it was impossible to clean them.

And so it was that Mrs Magic decided to put her plan into action. In her best cauldron, she brewed a potion of a thousand fresh slugs.

When the moon was full, in the dead of night, she went to whip up real magic. Her idea was to create the Great Storm.

She called to the rain. Then she called to the greatest force.

How the wind got up, and roared and howled! Lightning flashed, thunderbolts zoomed across the heavens, and the Great Storm took place. Just as Mrs Magic had planned.

In the Black Bat Hotel, people were woken by the terrible booming of thunder, the crack of lightning and a sense of big trouble to come.

The eighty-eight phones of the eighty-eight rooms added their alarming dinging to the noise outside.

In a final blast the Great Storm shook the hotel to its foundations. There was a massive power cut.

Chapter Six

As the hotel was plunged into darkness there was instant chaos. Guests who had barely left their rooms until now began stumbling down the Grand Staircase to reception. Puss, who could see in the dark, helped them on their way.

What Kind of hotel is this?
A magic hotel.
For heaven's sake, somebody do something.
magic lantern
Just one more step.
The Black Bat Hotel is pleased to issue these lanterns until power is restored.

During a lull in the storm, the guests turned to their computers.

There was a surprising number of guests for breakfast.

What's more, guests began to talk to each other, and children played together.

Puss and Partridge were very busy and Mrs Magic was happy at last.

In the calm of the evening Mrs Magic prepared to show her guests a thing or two about magic.

By slug, by snail, by mouse's tail,
Computers zoom to your rooms.
The Great Storm cut your power to zero,
Now, I'll show you a spell that's well...
twinkle
This should be good.

Eighty-eight computers whizzed into the sky and burst into a million stars.